I WAS RIGHT . . .

By lunch period every girl in the sixth grade knew about my secret admirer. I was passing the note around on the playground when Kim Baxter looked at me with admiration and said, "Wow! You've got two boys who like you, Randy Kirwan and now—HIM!"

It was obvious that most of the other girls were thinking that, too. Only Taffy Sinclair, who was standing near the edge of the crowd with Mona, looked unimpressed. Naturally, she was jealous. It served her right after the way she had flirted with Randy.

But suddenly she shot a poison-dart look in my direction and announced loudly, "If you ask me, Jana's secret admirer is probably some creep!" Then she whirled around and went stomping off with Mona trailing along behind her. It was all I could do to keep from laughing. She had just proved to everyone how jealous she really was.

TAFFY SINCLAIR AND THE SECRET ADMIRER EPIDEMIC

Betsy Haynes

A BANTAM SKYLARK BOOK®
TORONTO · NEW YORK · LONDON · SYDNEY · AUCKLAND

RL 5, 009–012

TAFFY SINCLAIR AND THE SECRET ADMIRER EPIDEMIC
A Bantam Skylark Book / March 1988

Skylark Books is a registered trademark of Bantam Books.
Registered in U.S. Patent and Trademark Office and elsewhere.

ISBN 0-553-15582-2

Published simultaneously in the United States and Canada

PRINTED IN THE UNITED STATES OF AMERICA

O   0 9 8 7 6 5 4 3 2

TAFFY SINCLAIR
AND THE
SECRET ADMIRER
EPIDEMIC

1 *

Some people think that if you have a boyfriend, all your troubles are over. Especially when that boyfriend is someone such as Randy Kirwan, the handsomest, kindest, and most sincere boy in the sixth grade at Mark Twain Elementary, not to mention the most popular. Well, Randy is my boyfriend, and I thought that all my troubles were over, too, until Monday after school. That's when one of my best friends, Melanie Edwards, came rushing up to my locker with her big news.

"Jana! Guess what! I've got a date!"

"WHAT!" I shouted over the sound of banging lockers and kids yelling in the hall. "What did you just say?"

"I said I have a *date*," Melanie gushed. Her face was pink from excitement, and her blue eyes were sparkling. "It's true. Scott Daly asked me to go to a movie with him on Saturday. His father is driving us. He says some of the other boys are going to get dates, too. There will be a bunch of kids going. I can't wait. It's going to be so romantic! You're going with Randy, aren't you?"

My other three best friends, Beth Barry, Katie Shannon, and Christie Winchell, had come up to us and were standing there, listening. It was like a slow-motion movie the way they turned to look at me. But I hardly noticed. My heart had thudded to the floor.

I shook my head. "He hasn't asked me . . . yet," I murmured.

"You're kidding," said Melanie with a shocked look on her face. "Scott passed me a note right under Wiggins's nose and asked me to go. I told him yes in the hall just now, right after the dismissal bell rang. He said Joel Murphy is taking Sara Sawyer, and Mark Peters asked Alexis Duvall before school this morning. Scott and Mark are Randy's two best friends, so you know if they're going, he is, too."

I didn't say anything. I couldn't. Why hadn't Randy asked me to go? It didn't make sense.

"Come on, Morgan. Brighten up," said Beth. "You know he'll ask you. He'll probably call you after he gets home from school. After all, he is your boyfriend."

I shrugged and tried to smile. Beth was right. He was my boyfriend, all right. I have had a mega-crush on him practically forever. For a while I even kept his picture hidden behind a poster of Miss Piggy on the wall beside my bed so that I could look at him in the glow of my night-light while I fell asleep. After ages and ages he finally noticed me, too, and asked me to go to his football game one Saturday and then to Mama Mia's for pizza afterward. A couple of weeks later, he walked me home from Mama Mia's, and then he kissed me. It was fantastic, and even though we haven't had another date, he always gave me his 1,000-watt smile every time he looked at me. He would surely ask me to the movie if his best friends were going. I was starting to feel better. I was certain he would call the minute I got home.

"I wonder why the boys want to take girls to a movie all of a sudden." said Katie.

I shrugged. I didn't care. I just wanted Randy to ask me.

"I don't have to be home until four-thirty," said Beth. "Do you want me to come over and help you wait for him to call?"

As soon as I nodded, Katie piped up, "I'll come, too."

"Me, too," said Melanie.

"Me, too," echoed Christie. "After all, we're The Fabulous Five. We stick together."

I couldn't help smiling at that. The Fabulous Five is a self-improvement club, and we meet every Saturday in my bedroom to try to find ways to become the most gorgeous and most popular girls in school. We even saved our dues for a while and had blue T-shirts made that say The Fabulous Five across the front in white letters, and we wear them to our meetings. We really are best friends, and we do stick together.

"Come on," I said. "Let's get going. My phone may be ringing off the wall."

The first thing I did when we got to my apartment was take the telephone off the end table by the sofa and set it squarely in the middle of the kitchen table where I could grab it the instant it rang. That was no problem because Mom had had an extra-long cord put on it so that she could talk on the phone while she worked in the kitchen. Then I pulled a bottle of soda out of the fridge and scrounged through the cupboards until I found a bag of chips. Since there were only four chairs at the table, Christie dragged in the desk chair from my bedroom, and then we all sat down at the table and stared at the phone.

"Come on, telephone. Hurry up and *ring*," I groaned.

Katie rolled her eyes in disgust. "It will never ring if you just sit here and wait for it. Don't you know that?"

I stuck out my tongue at her. Then I put an index finger at each of my temples, closed my eyes, and said, "I am sending an ESP message to Randy Kirwan. Come in, Randy Kirwan. Jana Morgan is home from school now. Pick up the telephone. Dial her number. Ask her to go to the movie with you Saturday. Over and out." I opened my eyes and grinned at my friends. "That should do it."

But the phone didn't ring. We finished the chips and drank our sodas and even ate all the ice cubes, but there wasn't so much as a peep from the telephone. It just sat there in the middle of the table, refusing to ring.

"What time is it? I have to be home at four-thirty," said Beth, as she put her empty glass in the sink.

I looked at my watch. "It's only five minutes until four. You still have lots of time."

"What are you going to do if he doesn't call?" asked Melanie.

"Why don't you call him?" asked Beth, as she dropped back into her chair. "Girls do that all the time, you know."

"I know," I murmured. I could feel my face turning red as I remembered the time I called Randy and disguised my voice by stuffing cotton balls into my cheeks. They made me gag so much that I almost threw up in the middle of our conversation. "I'd be embarrassed to call him. Besides, maybe he had to go somewhere after school. You know. Do an errand for his mom or something."

Christie was shaking her head slowly and on her face was a worried expression. "I don't know," she said softly. "Maybe I shouldn't mention this, but I saw Randy in the hall after lunch, and he was talking to Taffy Sinclair."

"What!" I shrieked. "Talking to Taffy Sinclair!? Why didn't you tell me before?"

"You don't really think he'd ask Taffy out instead of you, do you?" asked Katie. "Just because she flirts with him all the time. Everybody knows he's your boyfriend."

I didn't answer. All I could think of was Taffy Sinclair. Taffy is the most gorgeous girl in school, and she is my worst enemy in the world. We have hated each other practically forever, and she's always trying to take Randy Kirwan away from me. Taffy and I have had clubs against each other, and she even blackmailed me when I found our teacher's wallet after somebody else had stolen it and hidden it in the girls' bathroom. The only time we weren't enemies was when we found baby Ashley abandoned on the front steps of Mark Twain Elementary, but that special feeling between us only lasted a few days.

I closed my eyes and saw a picture in my mind of Randy talking to Taffy Sinclair in the hall after lunch. She was twirling a strand of her long blond hair and gazing at him with her big blue eyes. It made me want to die to see him pushing his dark wavy hair off his forehead and giving her the 1,000-watt smile he always gave to me. Just as he was starting to ask her to the movie, the phone rang, and I nearly jumped out of my skin.

"Oh, my gosh!" shrieked Melanie. "That's probably him!"

I swallowed hard and shot a hopeful glance at each of my friends. It had to be Randy. It just had to be. I started to reach for the receiver, but my hand was shaking so hard that I was afraid I'd drop it.

"Go ahead," urged Beth.

"What are you waiting for?" asked Katie. "It's probably him."

I nodded and grabbed the phone before I could chicken out again. "Hello?"

"Hi, honey." I slumped against the table. It was only Mom. "Just calling to tell you that I'm going to be a little late getting home from work. I'm going to stop by the cleaners and the grocery store."

"Sure, Mom," I mumbled, and hung up.

I put my elbows on the table and cupped my chin in my hands. Why didn't Randy call? Surely he would be home by this time. Was it possible that he had asked Taffy instead of me? I sat there watching the hands move slowly around the clock above the refrigerator. The later it got, the more worried I became. Finally it got so late that my friends started getting ready to go home.

"I still think you should call him yourself," grumbled Beth, as she began gathering her books and putting on her jacket.

"Me, too," said Christie.

"I'm not going to call him, and that's final."

"Okay, then I'll call him," challenged Beth.

"Don't you dare," I cried, feeling panicky. "Besides, he probably wouldn't tell you anything anyway. He knows you would tell me."

Melanie was standing by the door with her hand on the knob. Suddenly she let go of it and rushed to me. "I've got a great idea, Jana," she cried. "I'll have Scott find out what's going on. I'll have him ask Randy if he's going to take you to the movie, and I'll make Scott promise not to tell Randy who wants to know."

I didn't say anything for a moment. I wanted to find out what Randy was going to do more than anything in the world, but I was nervous, too.

"Well," I said slowly. "It might work, but you've got to make Scott *swear* he won't tell Randy that I'm the one who wants to know. If Randy ever found that out, I'd be so embarrassed that I'd die."

"Don't worry," said Melanie, giving me a confident smile. "Leave everything to me."

2 ❊

*T*he first thing I saw when I got to school the next morning made my heart start thumping like crazy. Melanie was by the bike racks, and she was talking to Scott.

I looked away fast. I would die if Scott saw me watching and figured out what was going on. Maybe it had been a mistake to let Melanie talk to him. Maybe Randy just hadn't gotten around to asking me, and if Scott started bugging him about it, he would change his mind. Good grief, I thought. Why had I let Melanie talk me into this?

Keeping my face turned straight ahead so that they wouldn't know I was watching, I looked at them out of the corner of my eye. They were still

11

talking. Why was it taking so long? I tried to read their lips, but I couldn't, and they were definitely too far away to hear.

I turned halfway toward them so that I could get a better look. Scott was smiling. In fact, he was laughing. What could Melanie possibly have said to make him laugh like that? Oh, my gosh, I thought. Did he think it was a big joke that Randy might ask me out again?

I wanted to die. That was probably it. Scott knew something that I didn't know. I closed my eyes and leaned against a tree, wishing that the ground would open up and swallow me. When I opened them again, Melanie was rushing toward me, grinning like crazy. My other three best friends had just gotten to school and were walking toward me, too.

"What did he say?" I demanded before Melanie could get a word out. "Does he know why Randy hasn't asked me out yet? And why was he laughing? Tell me every single word you said."

"Wow," Melanie said proudly. "Did I ever fake him out. He never suspected a thing."

"So?" I insisted. "What did you say?"

"Come on, Mel," groaned Katie. "Quit stalling."

"All I said was that I thought Saturday was going to be a lot of fun and I was glad so many kids were going. Then," Melanie paused and got a mysterious look on her face, "I *very casually* said, 'I suppose Randy is going, too. Is he taking Jana?'"

"Oh, my gosh!" I blurted. "What did he say?"

"He just shrugged and said he didn't know. And then I said, 'Would you ask him and let me know?' and he shrugged again and said, 'Sure.' That's all there was to it. As I said before, he didn't suspect a thing."

"So what was he laughing about?" I challenged. "Are you sure it wasn't about me?"

"Of course not, silly. We were just talking. It had nothing to do with you."

"Then why won't you tell us?"

"It was private. Did you tell everything that you and Randy talked about when he kissed you?" she teased.

My friends were grinning at me, and I could feel my ears getting hot and my face turning a brilliant shade of red. Naturally, I hadn't told them *everything*. Some things are just too personal to tell even your very best friends.

"Did you ask why all the boys are getting dates?" asked Katie.

Melanie frowned at her. "You don't really think I would ask Scott *why* he wants to take me to the movie, do you?"

Katie shrugged. Leave it to Katie, I thought, always putting a damper on things.

Just then Randy came screeching up to the bike racks.

"Look, Jana," cried Beth. "There he is."

I nodded and knelt down, pretending to be fixing my shoelace so that I could watch as he pushed his bike into a slot in the rack and locked it. Then he went racing over to Scott, and the two of them started horsing around.

"Rats!" I muttered. "That was a perfect opportunity for Scott to talk to him, but he blew it."

"Don't worry," Melanie insisted. "He'll do it. He said he would, didn't he?"

I shot her a dubious look and scuffed toward the school building. Sure, Melanie was convinced that Scott would talk to Randy, I thought miserably. But what if he didn't? Or what if he did—and found out that Randy didn't like me anymore? And wasn't going to ask me to the movie on Saturday? And was going to take Taffy Sinclair instead? What would I do then?

When I got to my locker, I opened the door and stared inside, thinking about that question. What *would* I do then? How would I face my friends? How would I face my number one enemy, Taffy Sinclair? I'd be so embarrassed that I'd die.

I got to our classroom ahead of Randy and was already in my seat when he came in. I was waiting for him to look at me and give me his 1,000-watt smile, but he didn't. He didn't turn around to look at me the way he sometimes did while Wiggins wrote the morning's math assignment on the board, either. I tried to tell myself that it was nothing to worry about. That just because he missed smiling at me one time, it wasn't the end of the world. But the truth is, that's how it felt.

During morning recess all the sixth-grade girls were talking about their dates for the movie. Alexis Duvall kept saying that Mark Peters was the cutest boy in the whole world and how she hoped that he would kiss her.

"Has Randy asked you yet?" Sara Sawyer asked. Everybody looked at me, including Taffy Sinclair, who was standing with Mona Vaughn at the edge of the group of girls.

I wanted to die. "Not yet," I mumbled.

"I wonder what he's waiting for?" asked Alexis. "Mark asked me yesterday."

"That's when Joel asked me, too," said Sara.

Taffy Sinclair got a nasty smile on her face. "Maybe Randy's going to ask someone else," she said.

I shrugged, trying to act as if it didn't matter, and moved away from the crowd. I didn't want to talk about it anymore. Especially to Taffy Sinclair. It was bad enough that he hadn't asked me yet. Did everybody have to make a big deal out of it, too?

I sat down on the front steps and gazed out across the playground, wishing recess would hurry up and be over. Just as Beth sat down beside me, I looked sharply at two boys by the drinking fountain. "Look," I whispered to Beth. "There are Scott and Randy over by the fountain. It looks as if they're talking about something serious."

"I'll bet it's you," said Beth.

I clutched Beth's arm. "Oh, my gosh. What will I do if Randy says he isn't going to ask me?"

"Relax. He's your boyfriend, isn't he? Of course he's going to ask you."

I exhaled a deep breath that I didn't realize I had been holding. "Sure," I murmured. "You're probably right."

I passed a note to Melanie the moment we were back inside and told her what I had seen. A few minutes later she passed one back that said she would talk to Scott at lunchtime and find out what

Randy had said. I glanced at the clock over the blackboard. Fifty-seven minutes until the lunch bell. More like fifty-seven years, I thought.

Wiggins marched us to the Media Center for free-reading period, which was the longest free-reading period I had ever lived through. I couldn't stand to sit at the reading tables or the typewriter or computer tables, where other kids could see how antsy I was, so I hid in the biography section and pretended to look for a book.

When I finally got to the cafeteria, I couldn't eat one single bite of my lunch. I kept pulling apart the halves of my cream cheese and jelly sandwich and sticking them back together. It was a dumb thing to do, but I was so nervous that I had to do something.

To make matters worse, the cafeteria was a madhouse. One table of fourth-graders was zinging peas back and forth at each other until Mr. Scott, the assistant principal, made them stop. Then he stood guard beside them and blocked our view of the table where Randy and Scott and all their friends were sitting.

Melanie must have seen the agony on my face. "Don't worry, Jana. I'm keeping an eye on the door. The minute I see Scott leave, I'll go talk to him."

I nodded and pulled my sandwich apart for the millionth time.

A few minutes later Melanie sprang to attention. "There he goes," she said, ducking down again and peering around Beth's shoulder at the door. "Okay, everybody. Give me a few minutes to talk to Scott and then meet me at our usual place beside the fence."

Katie and Beth and Christie and I all nodded. This was it. My stomach was churning so fast that I knew if I had eaten my lunch, I would throw it all up now.

My friends and I scrambled to clean our lunch things off the table and get out of the cafeteria. Then we hurried to the spot by the fence where we always meet when we want to talk about something private.

Melanie and Scott were standing by the building, and I hopped from one foot to the other as I watched them. "I wonder how long it will take her to talk to him?" I said.

Nobody answered, and a couple of minutes later Melanie headed in our direction. I couldn't help noticing that she wasn't smiling. In fact, she looked as if something were terribly wrong. "Oh, no," I whispered to myself.

"Did you ask him?" I demanded. "What did he say?"

Melanie took a deep breath. She looked so miserable that I knew what was coming before the first word was out of her mouth. "Scott said that he asked Randy if he was planning to take you to the movie Saturday, and he said no. Oh, Jana!" She rushed up and put her arms around me. "I can't believe it. He's your boyfriend!"

My friends all made sympathetic sounds and looked down at their feet. I could tell that they didn't know what to say. I just stood there, feeling as if my heart would burst. I didn't know what to say, either. What had happened? Why didn't Randy like me anymore? How could I possibly face *anybody* now?

"Is he taking Taffy?" I asked.

"I don't know," said Melanie. "Scott didn't say, but I could ask him if you want me to."

I shook my head. As badly as I wanted to know, I couldn't stand for Melanie to ask Scott. If he would tell her, he might blab it all over school.

I went inside the building when the bell rang and sank into my seat. I couldn't look toward Randy or at Wiggins when she announced the social studies assignment, and I could barely find the right page in my book. All I could think about was how I had to get away from school before everybody found out. If I could just get home, I could fake being sick. I could stay away for the rest of the year. Then next year, when everyone in my class had gone on to junior high, I could come back and finish sixth grade at Mark Twain Elementary.

I spent most of afternoon recess in the girls' bathroom, hiding out in one of the stalls. Even though my friends were sympathetic, they didn't know how I felt. They couldn't. No one could. Randy Kirwan wasn't going to take me to the movie on Saturday—which meant he didn't like me anymore. I was so miserable I thought I'd die.

When I got back to my seat after recess, there was a note lying on my desk. It looked like an ordinary note. White, lined notebook paper folded a jillion times, exactly like the notes The Fabulous Five passes back and forth in class whenever something really important happens.

Wiggins was writing spelling words on the blackboard so her back was turned while we got settled in our seats again. Before I opened the note, I looked at each of my four best friends to see if one of them had sent it. Maybe they had heard more news about Randy while I was in the girls' bathroom. Unfortunately, none of them was look-ing at me.

Then I thought about Randy. Maybe he had changed his mind and decided to ask me to the movie, after all. Maybe he had looked for me at recess, and when he couldn't find me on the playground, he had written a note and left it on my desk. But he wasn't looking at me, either.

Wiggins was still writing spelling words on the board, so I unfolded the note and spread it out on my desk. The first thing I noticed was that it was typed, but I forgot all about that as soon as I read what it said:

Dear Jana,

>*I am writing to tell you that I have been noticing you for a long time. I think you are very nice and very pretty.*
>*I know that you like Randy Kirwan, but I will keep hoping that someday you will like me instead.*

>*Your Secret Admirer*

I blinked a couple of times just in case I was dreaming and read it again. I caught my breath. It was true. I, Jana Morgan, had a secret admirer.

3 ✻

I sat at my desk as stiff as a statue thinking about
that note. I had folded it again so that no one could
peek over my shoulder and read it, but I could still
see the words in my mind: *Dear Jana, I have been
noticing you for a long time. . . .*

Thinking about those words made little tingles
race up and down my spine. Who was the note
from? He had to be in my class since he had left it
on my desk. And he was probably watching me the
very instant I read it.

"Jana Morgan! Pay attention, please."

I snapped to attention so fast that I bounced in
my seat. Wiggins was facing the class now, and she
was glaring at me over the tops of her wire-framed
glasses.

23

"The word you are to spell is 'unbelievable.'"

Un-be-liev-able, I thought, sounding out the syllables to myself. I looked down at my desk, feeling embarrassed. "Unbelievable" was from yesterday's spelling list. I had studied the words last night, but right now my mind was a total blank.

"We are all waiting," said Wiggins, and I heard someone behind me giggle.

"U-N," I began, "B-E-L-E-I—"

"You're forgetting the *I*-before-*E* rule," Wiggins interrupted sharply.

My ears were getting hot. The whole class was staring at me because I had forgotten the stupid old *I*-before-*E* rule—*I* before *E* except after *C*—and they were probably all thinking about how dumb I was. Randy Kirwan was staring, and all my friends were staring, and even my secret admirer was probably staring at me. MY SECRET AD-MIRER. I was so embarrassed I thought I'd die.

"U-N-B-E-L-I-E-V-A-B-L-E," I said. Then I went over the letters again in my mind to make sure I had been right this time.

"Thank you, Jana," Wiggins said. "Clarence Marshall. Spell 'pursuit.'"

I sank lower in my seat, relieved that everyone had taken his eyes off me and was now looking at

Clarence Marshall. But just as I was starting to relax, Taffy Sinclair turned around in her seat four desks in front of mine and gave me a nasty smile. I knew it was her way of saying that she would have spelled "unbelievable" right the first time. I shot a poison-dart look back at her and tried to concentrate on copying today's spelling words into my notebook, but it was hard. I couldn't help thinking about my secret admirer and wondering who he might be.

Nerd-of-the-world Curtis Trowbridge has had a crush on me for ages, but he has never tried to keep it a secret. Who else might it be? I looked around the room out of the corners of my eyes, first one direction and then the other. There were eleven boys in my class. Some of them, such as Keith Masterson and Scott Daly, were really cute. But some others, such as Clarence Marshall, were the pits.

Then I thought about Randy Kirwan. He was definitely cute and kind and sensitive, but he was a little bit conceited, too. I had learned that during the Romance Machine Disaster. I liked him anyway, but still it would serve him right for dumping me if he found out that I had a secret admirer. And Randy had never done anything as romantic as writing me a note such as the one I had just gotten. I darted a quick glance at him. He was looking down at a paper on his desk. He has probably forgotten that I even exist, I thought.

I could hardly wait for school to be dismissed so that I could show my four best friends the note.

"What!" shrieked Beth the minute we were far enough away from the school ground for me to tell them without someone else's overhearing. "You're kidding! A secret admirer? How do you know?!"

"Here," I said slyly. Then I slowly extracted the note from my jeans pocket. "This was on my desk when I got in from afternoon recess. Read it yourselves."

Katie gave me a disgusted look as if to say that anything to do with boys was too gross for words, but she snatched the note just as Beth's hand shot out to grab it for herself. Katie unfolded it and read it without comment, and then passed it on.

Melanie sighed loudly and fluttered her eyelids. "Oh, Jana, it's so romantic." Then she got a puzzled look on her face. "It's sort of strange that your secret admirer decided to send you this note today. I mean, everybody in the sixth grade is talking about Saturday and all the kids who have dates. Do you think he is getting up his nerve to ask you out for Saturday, too?"

"Melanie, you're a genius," shouted Christie. "That has to be it."

"Right," said Beth. "He was probably watching you when you read the note to see your reaction. Now think. Did you smile or get a dreamy look on your face or anything?"

"I can't remember," I confessed. "I was so surprised. When I first saw the note lying on my desk I thought that one of you sent it. Then I sort of hoped it was from Randy and that he had changed his mind about asking me out. Then when I saw that it was from a secret admirer, I couldn't believe my eyes."

"And did you notice that it's typed? Maybe he's older," said Christie. "I mean, most kids don't type. They write notes in pencil or ballpoint pen."

I knew instantly why Christie had said that. Her mother, Mrs. Winchell, is the principal of our school, and Christie has had this mega-crush on Mr. Scott, the new assistant principal, since the beginning of the school year.

"It's from a kid, all right," I assured her. "Just look at all the crossed-out letters."

"Well, he sounds mature," insisted Christie. "Immature little kids don't write love letters."

"Whoever he is, he must be pretty shy to send you a note instead of talking to you in person," said Katie.

"Not necessarily," I countered. "After all, he said that he knew I liked Randy Kirwan, so he probably thought he didn't stand a chance."

"Tomorrow I think we should all keep our eyes peeled to see if we can spot any boy who is looking at Jana a lot," said Beth.

"Good idea," said Melanie. "If he likes her enough to send her a secret admirer note, he probably can't take his eyes off her. That should make it easy to find out who he is."

"Well, I just hope that he's somebody really cute who will make Randy Kirwan so-o-o-o jealous when he finds out that he will practically go berserk!" said Beth. "That would serve him right."

"Yeah," I whispered as a shimmery feeling went through me. It was getting more exciting by the minute.

My friends and I talked for a little while longer, making plans to be detectives at school the next day and find out who my secret admirer was. After I got home I spread the note on the kitchen table and studied it for a long time. I was thinking about all the detective shows I had seen on television where the bad guy types a note on a typewriter with a crooked letter, and as soon as they find the typewriter, they know who he is and arrest him. Unfortunately, there weren't any crooked letters in this note. All I could hope for was that he would stare at me a lot tomorrow.

4 ✻

I could hardly wait for Mom to get home from work so that I could show her my secret admirer note. I wondered if she would have any suggestions for finding out who he was. I had been racking my brain and hadn't come up with one single idea.

When I heard her come into the apartment, I grabbed the note and went to meet her.

"Hi, sweetheart," she chirped. "Wait until you see what I have."

I couldn't imagine what she was talking about. As soon as she hung up her coat, she began pulling brightly colored brochures out of her purse and spreading them on the kitchen table.

"Just look at this." She thrust a flyer toward me with a beautiful lady in a bathing suit on the front.

"Bermuda! And here's one for Disney World in Florida."

I stuffed my secret admirer note into my back pocket and took the brochure, but I didn't look at it. All these vacation flyers could mean only one thing. "Are you and Pink planning your honeymoon?" I said around the lump that was growing in my throat.

Pink is short for Wallace Pinkerton, and he and my mother are engaged. I like Pink a lot, but it's hard for me to think of him as part of our family since my father lives less than one hundred miles away in Poughkeepsie, New York. Of course, he's an alcoholic and never comes to see me or very seldom writes, but still, he's the one who is really my father, not Pink.

Mom got a surprised look on her face. "Oh, no, honey," she insisted. "These have nothing to do with Pink and me. We haven't even set a wedding date yet. They're for us. I should have explained."

I was more confused than ever. "What do you mean, they're for us? We could never go places like these. They're EXPENSIVE!"

I shook my head. It was no secret that we had trouble getting by on what Mom made as classified ad manager at the *Bridgeport Post*, especially when my father didn't send the monthly support check.

There was certainly no way that we could afford to go to a place like Disney World.

"I know," Mom admitted. "But I walk by a travel agency every day on my way to and from work, and the pictures on their windows always look so exciting. I just thought it might be fun to look at some of their brochures and pretend that we were going on a big adventure." Then she grinned sheepishly and said, "That was sort of silly, wasn't it?"

"Gosh, no. I'd love to go on an exciting vacation. Maybe if we started saving change in an empty jar we could go someday."

Mom laughed and gave me a hug. Then she picked up the brochures and dropped them into the wastebasket. "That's a good idea. I even have an empty mayonnaise jar we can use. Let's see how much we save before we start planning," she said cheerfully. "Now you finish your homework while I get supper started."

When I got back to my room, I opened my math book, but I couldn't concentrate on the problems. I was thinking about Mom. I had never realized what a boring life she led. No wonder she was crabby sometimes. She just went to work every day and then came home and cooked dinner and took care of me. Oh, sure, she had Pink. But he wasn't exactly Mr. Excitement. He's a supernice man, and he's a printer at the same newspaper where Mom works, but that's about it. He's also a bowling nut, and he takes Mom bowling at the very same bowling alley every single Saturday night. It's no wonder that she was dreaming of exciting places.

Just then I remembered that I had forgotten to show Mom the note from my secret admirer. I started to get up and go back to the kitchen, but I stopped in midair. I sank into my chair again, feeling a little guilty. Having a secret admirer was pretty exciting, and poor Mom was dying for some excitement in her life. Wasn't that why she had brought home all those brochures? Maybe I should wait awhile to show it to her, at least until we had a little change in our vacation jar.

❊ ❊ ❊

The next morning Christie met me a block from school. She looked as if she were dying of excitement.

"You're going to love this," she said, balancing her notebook on one knee and flipping it open. "Here." She pointed to a page with some names written on it. "I've made a list of every boy in our class, eleven boys to be exact. Then I've made blanks for every period of the day, every recess, and even lunch period. I'll give one of these lists to each member of The Fabulous Five, and we can each make a check in the right blank every time a boy looks at you during the day. That way, at the end of the day, we'll be able to see exactly who has been looking at you the most. Isn't it great?"

Christie didn't wait for me to answer. She removed the top sheet and handed it to me proudly. I know my mouth was hanging open, but I couldn't help it. Leave it to Christie. She is a mathematical genius and loves figuring things out. She had even made the lists on graph paper so that all the blanks were exactly the same size.

"Wow," I said. "This is really great."

"I thought so, too," she said confidently. "And with each one of us keeping track of every single boy, we shouldn't miss any important glances or stares."

A couple of minutes later the rest of our friends walked up, and I read over the list of boys while she explained her plan to them.

1. Randy Kirwan
2. Scott Daly
3. Mark Peters
4. Clarence Marshall
5. Curtis Trowbridge

6. Joel Murphy
7. Keith Masterson
8. Richie Corrierro
9. Gregory Harper
10. Eric Silverman
11. Matt Zeboski

"Of course, Randy Kirwan can be eliminated immediately," I huffed. "I'm going to cross him off the list as soon as I get to my desk."

"Well, what about Scott?" Melanie asked indignantly. "Surely nobody thinks he's the secret admirer."

"And Joel has already asked Sara, and Mark asked Alexis," added Beth.

"Come on, you guys," Christie pleaded. "I wrote down every boy in the class just to make sure I didn't leave anybody out. It isn't going to hurt anything."

Melanie gave Christie a frosty look and then made a big ceremony of folding her sheet and sticking it into her social studies book. It was obvious that her feelings were hurt, and I crossed my fingers behind my back that we wouldn't all be mad at each other before this mystery was solved.

I stopped off in the girls' bathroom to brush my hair before I went to class. I wanted to make sure

that I looked my very best for my secret admirer—
whoever he was. I was also thinking about the
eleven boys in my class. Four of them had been
eliminated right away—Randy, Scott, Mark, and
Joel—so that left only seven. In my mind I went
down the list of the ones who were left. Clarence
Marshall, jerk. Curtis Trowbridge, nerd. Keith
Masterson, cute! Richie Corrierro, cute! Gregory
Harper, too quiet. Eric Silverman, semicute. Matt
Zeboski, almost semicute. One of those seven had
to be my secret admirer.

Next I eliminated Clarence, Curtis, and Gregory. I would die if it turned out to be any of them. I
was down to four. Ranking them on the cute scale,
Keith was first, Richie was second, Eric was third,
and Matt, fourth. Now, I wondered, where do I go
from here?

5 ✳

When the bell rang and I slid into my seat a few minutes later, I thought about Mom. She was probably sitting at her desk at the *Bridgeport Post* doing her boring job, and here I was at my desk at Mark Twain Elementary trying to figure out which boy in my class was my secret admirer. I couldn't help feeling sorry for her, and I promised myself that I would think of something to make her life as exciting as mine.

While Wiggins took roll and made the morning announcements, I checked my sweater pocket to make sure my secret admirer note was still there. Then I took the chart with the names of the eleven sixth-grade boys out of my notebook and slid it under my math book, where I could get to it in a hurry as soon as boys started looking at me. I glanced around quickly to see if any were yet, but they weren't.

Randy was drawing something on a sheet of paper, and when I looked at him, I had a hard time looking away. He was so kind and sensitive, so sincere, the most wonderful boy in the world. What had I done? Why had he changed his mind about me? Surely if he still liked me, he would be taking me to the movie on Saturday.

Just then I had the feeling that someone was looking at me. I sucked in my breath, but I didn't dare move. It might be my secret admirer. Sitting perfectly rigid, I walked two fingers over to the chart sticking out from under my math book and gradually drew it out until all the names were showing. Then, with my other hand, I rolled my pencil down my desk into my lap and grabbed hold of it. Finally, I moved my head very slowly to first the right and then the left until I spotted him. Keith Masterson! My heart did a flip-flop. He was the cutest boy in the class—next to Randy Kirwan, of course—and he was looking straight at me.

I didn't know if I should smile or what I should do, but before I could make up my mind, Keith looked away. Oh, well, I thought. He'll probably look at me again if he's my secret admirer. Then I found the line beside Keith's name on the chart and made an X in the box for first period.

I felt a tap on my shoulder. "Jana, I need to borrow a pencil," Clarence Marshall whispered, so loudly that I'm sure Wiggins heard it all the way up at her desk.

I turned around and glared at him. I didn't want to get into trouble, so I made the words with my lips but didn't make a sound. "I didn't bring any extras."

Of course, Clarence couldn't read lips. "What?" he whispered even louder.

In desperation I handed him my pencil. I could write with my ballpoint pen. Then a terrible thought occurred to me. Should I make an X by Clarence's name? He had not only looked at me, he had gotten my attention. Isn't that what you do when you like someone? Rats! I thought. Looking around, I could see that my four best friends were all concentrating on their math problems. Probably none of them had noticed Clarence bugging me. I smiled slyly to myself. No one would ever have to know.

Just then I caught another pair of eyes looking in my direction. Scott Daly. Yipes, I thought. He was staring straight at me and he didn't look away when I stared back. I knew I had to make an X by his name, but what would Melanie say? She was already mad about Scott's name being on the list. Well, I thought indignantly, she would just have to understand. We were doing this in a very scientific manner, and naturally my secret admirer wouldn't be the only person in the entire universe who ever looked at me.

I kept my head down and peeked at Randy again. He was still drawing. It seemed as if everyone were looking at me except him. I glanced at the clock above the blackboard. It had only been ten minutes since the bell, and I had already been looked at by two boys, three if you counted Clarence Marshall. I couldn't help feeling pleased. I had never realized before just how popular I really was. Probably boys looked at me all the time, and I just didn't know it. Randy Kirwan wasn't the only boy in the world.

By morning recess, I had four X's on my chart. Scott Daly had looked at me once, Richie Corrierro once, Matt Zeboski once, and Keith Masterson. Unfortunately Keith had only looked at me once, also, but I hadn't given up hope that he was my secret admirer.

My friends and I all raced to our special spot by the fence to compare charts. Everyone wanted to talk first.

"Matt Zeboski has looked at you three times!" cried Katie.

"Three times?" I said in disbelief. Matt was okay, but he was pretty far down on the cute scale. "I only saw him look at me once."

"That's because you don't sit as close to him as I do," said Katie. "I can see every move he makes."

"I saw him look at you twice," said Beth. "And I have to twist around to see him."

"Okay," I conceded. "Three for Matt Zeboski. How many times did anyone see Keith Masterson looking at me?"

"None," said Christie.

"Nope. None for me, either," said Beth.

Katie and Melanie were shaking their heads, also. Then Beth shook her head without looking at me. She wasn't smiling.

"Well, he looked at me at least once," I blurted. "You guys should keep your eyes open."

"This is fun," said Christie. "Maybe I'll make a chart to keep track of how many times Mr. Scott looks at me." She laughed.

Melanie didn't say anything when I mentioned that Scott Daly had looked at me, but I had the feeling that she didn't like it. Christie suggested that we copy each other's charts so that we all had the same X's in the same blanks. When we finished there were a total of six: one for Scott Daly, one for Keith Masterson, one for Richie Corrierro, and THREE for Matt Zeboski. Fortunately, no one had seen Clarence talking to me, but then no one had seen Randy Kirwan looking at me, either, and that was the pits.

I was leaning against the fence gazing into space and thinking about all the attention I was getting from boys when my eyes suddenly came sharply into focus. "Hey, guys, look," I said. "Do you see what I see? Randy is talking to Taffy Sinclair."

Everybody followed my gaze. "Oh, no!" said Melanie in a whiny voice. "Oh, Jana. That's awful."

It was awful. Taffy was smiling her icky sweet smile at him and talking a mile a minute. Randy wasn't saying anything, but he was looking at her and giving *her* his 1,000-watt smile.

"I wonder what they're talking about?" asked Beth.

The rest of us shrugged, but I knew that they were all thinking the same thing I was. Taffy knew that Randy hadn't asked me to go to the movie on Saturday, and she was flirting with him so he would ask her!

I sucked in my breath. Now Randy was talking, and Taffy was smiling bigger than ever and nodding. Nodding?! That was the same as saying yes! Oh, no, I thought, closing my eyes. My worst fears had come true.

"Are you sure you don't want me to ask Scott what's going on?" asked Melanie. "You know, if Randy still likes you, if he's taking Taffy to the movie, stuff like that?"

"No," I said sharply. I couldn't let on that I'd be too embarrassed for Scott to tell her things such as that. What if he told her that Randy thinks I'm a jerk and that he adores Taffy? What would I do then?

"I have a better idea," I said, as one suddenly popped into my mind. "I'm going to tell everybody about my secret admirer."

"What good is that going to do?" asked Katie.

"Think about it. I'll bet if Randy knew I have a secret admirer he would be jealous. He is too conceited. He wouldn't be able to stand it if he knew he was losing me to another boy."

"Hey, you're right," shouted Beth. "Besides, it will be fun to tell the other girls and see the looks on their faces."

There was another reason I wanted to tell everybody about my secret admirer, too, but I didn't say it out loud. It would help me face all the other kids if Randy really did dump me for Taffy Sinclair.

"Come on," I said. "There's Alexis over there, and she's talking to Lisa and Sara. Once we tell them, every kid in Mark Twain Elementary will know about it by noon."

6 *

I was right. By lunch period every girl in sixth grade knew about my secret admirer. I was passing the note around on the playground when Kim Baxter looked at me with admiration and said, "Wow! You've got two boys that like you, Randy Kirwan and now—HIM!"

It was obvious that most of the other girls were thinking that, too. Marcie Bee rolled her eyes toward the sky and acted as if she were going to faint. She probably would have fallen if her two best friends, Gloria Drexler and Mary Sweeney, hadn't caught her. Lisa and Sara and Alexis were grinning at me as if I were someone special, and I heard Stephanie Holgrem ask Melanie when I had

47

gotten the note. Only Taffy Sinclair, who was standing near the edge of the crowd with Mona, looked unimpressed. Naturally, she was jealous. It served her right after the way she had flirted with Randy. But suddenly she shot a poison-dart look in my direction and announced loudly, "If you ask me, Jana's secret admirer is probably some creep!" Then she whirled around and went stomping off with Mona trailing along behind her. It was all I could do to keep from laughing. She had just proved to everyone how jealous she really was.

"Does Randy know about the secret admirer note yet?" asked Sara.

"Not that I know of," I said, as casually as I could. "But he'll probably hear about it."

"I'll bet he'll be jealous," said Lisa.

"I'll bet he will, too," said Kim.

He'd better be jealous! I thought, but I didn't say it out loud. I wondered how long it would be before he got the news. Not long, I hoped. This was already Wednesday, and the movie was only three days away. He had to hear about it pretty soon or else he wouldn't have time to get jealous enough to ask me to go.

The afternoon dragged by. I didn't see anyone talking to Randy, and he didn't turn around and look at me or anything so he probably didn't know yet. I did make some more X's on my chart, though. Curtis Trowbridge looked at me twice. Mark Peters and Joel Murphy each looked at me once. And Keith Masterson looked at me four whole times!

Keith was definitely ahead. He had five X's. The only other boy coming close was Matt Zeboski with three. Keith was probably my secret admirer. That was why he couldn't keep his eyes off me. The idea made me tingly. He was awfully cute. He had blond hair and a really neat smile. I would rather have Keith for a boyfriend than anyone, except Randy, of course.

I wondered if Keith would ask me to the movie. Surely he wasn't too shy. He probably just didn't want to hurt Randy's feelings. Well, I thought, Randy had better just watch out. I might decide that I liked Keith better anyway.

I was daydreaming about Keith and me at the movie when the recess bell rang. I grabbed my chart as I headed for the playground. I wanted to be sure my friends knew that Keith had looked at me five times today.

"I only saw him looking at you twice," said Katie. "But Eric Silverman was looking at you. I saw him once and a half."

"Once and a half?" I shrieked. "How can somebody look at you one and a half times?"

"He started to look at you, and then Joel poked him to borrow a sheet of paper," Katie explained.

"Oh, brother," I muttered.

"I only saw Keith look at you once," said Beth. "I also saw Matt Zeboski looking at you again. That makes four times for him. Matt must be your secret admirer."

I sighed. I didn't want to talk about Matt. "Didn't anybody else see Keith look at me four times?" I pleaded.

My friends all shook their heads.

Before we went in, we totaled up each boy. Even though I was the only one who had seen him looking at me so much, I made sure they all knew that Keith led with five times. Next was Matt with four. Curtis Trowbridge was third with two. Eric Silverman was fourth with one and a half, and Scott, Mark, Joel, and Richie each had one. I was dying to grin or dance in circles or do something silly, even though Randy hadn't looked at me once. That was a grand total of sixteen and a half times a boy had looked at me today, and the day wasn't even over. I had never realized that I was so popular.

The moment I got back into the classroom from recess, I saw another note on my desk. I swallowed hard and hurried over to pick it up. It's probably just a note from one of my friends, I reasoned. But I knew that all of my best friends had been with me on the playground, and none of them had said anything about passing me a note.

I glanced around to see if anyone was watching me. Randy was looking out the window, and Keith was still coming in the door. I didn't dare look at Matt Zeboski or any of the other boys. If one of them were looking at me, I'd die.

I could tell the minute I started unfolding it that it was from my secret admirer because it was typed. I practically tore it getting it open. It said:

Dear Jana,

Roses are red,
Violets are blue.
Wow! Have I got
A crush on you!!!

                    Your Secret Admirer

P.S. Do you like movies?

Oh, my gosh! I thought. It was too wonderful to be true. Keith was thinking about asking me to the movie on Saturday. What could I do to let him know that the answer to his question was yes?

7 ❋

*F*or the rest of the afternoon I racked my brain, trying to come up with a way to let Keith know that I liked movies. I thought about asking Melanie to talk to Scott again, but that would be embarrassing. He'd think I was some kind of nut, first wanting to know if Randy was going to take me to the movie and then asking him to tell Keith that I like movies. There had to be a better way.

I also thought about getting my four best friends to help me. We could stand near Keith on the playground tomorrow, and as soon as I thought he was listening to our conversation, I could say in a really loud voice, "I just love movies!" But that would be dumb, too. There had to be something else I could do. But what?

I didn't have to wonder long. When I got to my locker after school, there was *another* note sticking in the door. It was folded, just like the other two, and the minute I started opening it I could see it was typed. I was so excited that my hands were shaky, and I held my breath, hoping that Keith had signed his name this time. He hadn't, but it didn't matter. The instant I read that note I knew he was going to ask me out.

Dear Jana,

If you like movies, wear something red tomorrow.

Your Secret Admirer

I jerked the locker door open, pitched my social studies book in, grabbed my math book since I had math homework, slammed the door, and danced off down the hall to find my friends. I could hardly wait to show them this latest development in the secret admirer case. I chuckled to myself. That was what a detective would say. I felt like a detective and a pretty good one at that. I was sure I knew who my secret admirer was, and now I was certain that he was going to ask me to the movie on

Saturday. All I had to do was wear something red to school tomorrow.

My friends were excited, too. All except Katie, of course.

"Wow! This is really terrific," said Melanie. "Maybe we can double. Wouldn't that be fun? Scott and me, and you and your secret admirer."

"Me and Keith," I corrected.

"You still don't know for sure that it's Keith," insisted Katie.

"He's the one who looks at me the most," I said. "That proves he likes me, and I'm going to wear my red jumpsuit tomorrow to let him know that I like movies."

Katie sighed and looked at me as if I were the dumbest person alive. "If he's shy enough to send you notes signed 'Your Secret Admirer' instead of talking to you in person, then he's probably too shy to look at you in class, too. If you ask me, it's probably Gregory Harper."

"Gregory Harper!" I shrieked. "He's the quietest boy in our class. He's probably the quietest boy in the universe. He never looks at girls."

"That's why I think he's your secret admirer," Katie said smugly. "He likes you and he's trying to get up his courage to ask you out."

Christie made a face at Katie. "I agree with you, Jana. I think it's Keith, and he's just testing you with all this secret admirer stuff to see if you and Randy still like each other. After all, they are friends, and he probably doesn't want to hurt Randy's feelings."

"That's what I think, too," said Melanie.

I headed home, feeling like the luckiest and most popular girl in the world. So what if Randy didn't like me anymore? Taffy could flirt with him if she wanted to. I had Keith Masterson now.

I could hardly wait for Mom to get home. I was definitely going to show her my notes this time. I knew she would be just as excited as I was. I spread them out on the kitchen counter where she would be sure to see them. Then I thought about her situation again. Poor Mom. Why didn't Pink ever take her to a movie instead of bowling every Saturday night? It had to be the most boring thing in the world. She never complained, but then she never said she really liked to bowl, either.

Pink was awfully nice, but it was a shame that Mom didn't have any other boyfriends. I couldn't remember her ever going out with anyone else since she and my father were divorced when I was three. And she was engaged to marry Pink! Maybe he wasn't the right one for her at all, but how would she ever know that if she never went out with anyone else?

Then I got this great idea. Mom needed a secret admirer to put a little excitement in her life. I thought about that for a moment. I didn't know any single guys except Pink. If I did, maybe I could talk them into writing her notes. *Eeek!* I thought. I could never do a thing such as that. But there was one thing that I could do. I could send her secret admirer notes myself. It would only be sort of cheating. They wouldn't be from a real secret admirer, but they might make her life more fun and convince her that she ought to look around a little before she married Pink.

The more I thought about my great idea, the better I liked it. I could start by copying the first note I had gotten. That would be easy. I scooped up my notes from the kitchen counter and raced to my desk.

Dear Patricia,

No, I thought. That was too formal.

Dear Pat,

I am writing to tell you that I have been noticing you for a long time. I think you are very nice and very pretty.

I know that you like Wallace Pinkerton, but I will keep hoping that someday you will like me instead.

Your Secret Admirer

Wow! I thought. That was great. But if I wrote it, even printed it, she would recognize my handwriting. I would have to type it. We didn't have a typewriter at home, but there was one in the Media Center at school. Kids could use it anytime they wanted to. I looked at my watch. It was only five after three. The school would still be open for after-school activities such as Girl Scouts and for teachers getting their rooms ready for tomorrow. If I hurried, I could get there, type the note, and leave it in our mailbox—all before Mom got home from work.

8 *

I grabbed my notebook and went racing off to Mark Twain Elementary. I took my notebook along because I didn't know how many pieces of paper I would have to use before I got the note typed without any mistakes. I couldn't just run a slash mark through wrong letters the way Keith had done my notes. Mom's note would have to be perfect.

When I got to the Media Center, Mrs. Birney, the librarian, was shelving books. She looked surprised to see me, but she smiled and waved for me to come in.

"Would it be all right if I used the typewriter for a few minutes?" I hoped she wouldn't ask me what I was going to type.

59

Fortunately, she didn't. She just nodded and smiled again.

As soon as I rolled a sheet of paper into the typewriter, I had a terrible thought. It was regular, lined notebook paper. Grown men who wrote secret admirer notes to beautiful women wouldn't use lined notebook paper. They would use expensive stationery. Maybe even stationery that smelled like perfume. I sighed and looked at the paper in the machine. It was all I had. Not only that, I couldn't afford to go out and buy expensive stationery that smelled like perfume. My own stationery at home had kittens on it. Grown men would never write secret admirer notes to beautiful women on stationery with kittens on it, either.

I sighed and started to type. The first mistake I made was forgetting to capitalize *D* and *P* in "Dear Pat." I wrote "dear pat." I made a face and pulled the paper out of the machine. Then I rolled a second sheet in and started again. This time I got all the way to "noticing" before I made a mistake. I was glad Wiggins wasn't there to see that I forgot to drop the *e* off notice" before adding the "ing."

By the time I finally finished, I had used six sheets of paper. Typing was pretty hard. I didn't know how Mom did it all day long. I put the note into my notebook and thanked Mrs. Birney as I left. It was getting late. I would have to hurry to get home and plant the note in the mailbox before Mom got there. I wished that I could mail it, but I didn't have a stamp. Plus, I was too anxious for Mom to get it. I couldn't stand to wait a day or two for it to go through the mail.

I was almost to the front door of the school when I heard someone call my name. It was Mrs. Winchell, the school principal, and when I turned toward her, she was smiling. "Hi, Jana. What are you doing at school so late?"

"I just needed to use the typewriter in the Media Center." I liked Mrs. Winchell. For a principal she was pretty nice. Besides that, she was Christie's mother, and Christie was one of my best friends.

"I hear that you got a note from a secret admirer."

My heart stopped. "How did you hear about that?"

"Miss Wiggins told me. News such as that travels around the school pretty fast."

"Oh," I said, relaxing a little. I had thought at first that maybe she knew who my secret admirer was. "Actually, I've gotten three notes. The last one was stuck in my locker door after school."

"Well, that's pretty exciting."

I nodded, and a big grin spread across my face.

"Have you figured out who he is yet?"

I nodded again. "I think so, anyway. There's one boy in class that looked at me five times today. I think it's him."

"That sounds like a good possibility to me. By the way, do you have the notes with you?"

"No, they're at home."

Mrs. Winchell's smile faded and she looked thoughtful for a moment. "Would you bring them into the office in the morning and let me look at them? It seems that you aren't the only one at Mark Twain Elementary who has gotten a note from a secret admirer."

My mouth must have dropped open at the news because Mrs. Winchell laughed nervously and added, "There is probably no connection between this other person's secret admirer and yours, but I would like to compare the notes just to make sure. I hope you won't mind."

I said that I would bring them and then headed for home. I was totally stunned. Another secret admirer sending notes to someone in our school? The closer I got to our apartment, the more worried I became. What if someone was playing a trick? Sending secret admirer notes to lots of people and then watching to see what they did?

But if lots of kids were getting secret admirer notes, why hadn't I heard about them?

A block from home I stopped and leaned against a tree. I had just had another terrible thought. My secret admirer had said to wear red to school tomorrow if I like movies. I had planned to wear my red jumpsuit and red socks and maybe even red barrettes in my hair. What if my secret admirer was the same one who had been sending notes to other kids? And what if a bunch of us showed up tomorrow wearing red? Then whoever was playing a trick on us would have a big laugh.

That settled it. I would *not* wear red to school tomorrow. Not even if everything else I owned was dirty. I would never wear red to school again for as long as I lived. But instead of being angry, I wanted to cry. I had been so sure that Keith Masterson was my secret admirer.

I thought about the notes again and all the times that Keith had looked at me today. He had to be my secret admirer. He just had to! Maybe someone had heard about my secret admirer and decided to write a note to someone they liked. Surely that was it. I tried to remember what Mrs. Winchell had said. She had said that I wasn't the only one who had a secret admirer. She didn't say that lots of people had them. In fact I remembered her saying something about "this other person's secret admirer." And what if I didn't wear red tomorrow? And my secret admirer really was Keith? And he thought I didn't like movies? He wouldn't ask me to go with him Saturday!

I couldn't help wondering who the other person with a secret admirer was. I knew that if it were any of my four best friends I would know about it. And it wouldn't be Alexis Duvall or Sara Sawyer. They both had dates for Saturday. Taffy Sinclair! It had to be her. Boys were always looking at her and saying how pretty she was. Probably some boy who was too shy to talk to her had heard about my secret admirer and decided to send her a note. Maybe her secret admirer was Gregory Harper, the shy kid who Katie felt certain was sending my notes. I had to giggle at that. It would serve Taffy right. But what if it wasn't? And what if it wasn't someone playing tricks, either? What if it turned out to be Randy Kirwan and he was planning to ask her to the movie on Saturday?

I trudged on home, feeling more confused than ever. There was only one thing I felt certain of. I had to leave the secret admirer note I had just typed in the mailbox where Mom would find it. Since I was the one who wrote it, I knew that no one was playing a trick on her. Well, not really, anyway.

9 ❀

I opened the mailbox and slipped Mom's secret admirer note in between an envelope with a window in it that was probably a bill and a magazine and hurried upstairs to wait for her. I couldn't sit still, even though she was due home any minute. I spread my homework out on my desk, but I couldn't get started on it. I checked twice to see if my red jumpsuit was clean. It was. My red socks were, too. I checked them three times.

Finally I heard her key turning in the lock. I hurried into the kitchen before she got inside and leaned against the counter, trying to look casual.

"Hi, sweetheart," she called as she came in, and pitched the mail onto the sofa without looking at it. "How was your day?"

Rats! I thought, but I gave her a big smile and said, "Great. How was yours?"

"Okay, but busy."

She still didn't look at the mail. I had to think of something.

"Any interesting mail?" I asked, still trying to appear casual.

"I don't know. I haven't looked at it yet. You can check it if you want to, but it's probably all bills. That's all we ever get around this time of month."

I looked down at the assortment of junk mail and other stuff fanned out across the sofa cushion. I could see one corner of the folded sheet of lined notebook paper peeking out, and I got a tingly feeling. I wanted *her* to pick up the mail and thumb through it and find the secret-admirer note herself.

Mom hung up her coat and headed for the kitchen. When she passed the sofa she gave the mail a disgusted look and said, "All bills, right?" Then she walked on by.

I knew I had to take action. I scooped up the letters and followed her into the kitchen. "I haven't looked yet. Hey, look at this. It's the phone bill."

Mom turned around and gave me a quizzical look. At that instant I pulled the secret-admirer note out and waved it toward her. "I wonder what this is?" Before she could answer, I pushed it into her hand.

Shrugging, Mom unfolded the lined notebook paper and frowned as she read. "My secret admirer?" she whispered. "This has to be some kind of joke."

"Secret admirer?" I asked, trying to fake surprise.

My heart was racing as she handed me the note. I cleared my throat and read the message out loud. "'Dear Pat, I am writing to tell you that I have been noticing you for a long time. I think you are very nice and very pretty. I know that you like Wallace Pinkerton, but I will keep hoping that someday you will like me instead.' Signed, 'Your Secret Admirer.' Wow! Mom, you have a secret admirer! Isn't it exciting?"

Mom rolled her eyes toward the ceiling and took the note back, only instead of reading it again, she pitched it into the wastebasket. "It's probably some kook," she said angrily. "Just look at it. It's typed and on notebook paper at that. There's no envelope. No stamp. It *has* to be a kook. Jana," she said, putting both hands on my shoulders and looking me straight in the eye, "I want you to be *very careful* walking back and forth to school. Don't talk to strangers. And be alert for anyone loitering in the hallway of this apartment building. There are a lot of crazies out there in the world, and we've apparently gotten the attention of one of them."

I blinked hard. "But Mom—" I started to protest.

Mom cut me off. "There are no buts about it, Jana. I've lived longer than you have, and I know that this could be dangerous. I want you to do exactly what I've told you. That's all there is to it."

I scuffed off to my room with my heart in my throat. I was only trying to put some excitement into Mom's life. Some romance. But I had goofed it up, and now she was scared half to death that we were being stalked by some kind of creep.

10 ✳

I took my red jumpsuit out of the closet the next morning and laid it across my bed. Should I wear it or not? Then I got out my red socks and put them next to the jumpsuit. It was one of my favorite outfits. So what if I just happened to wear it today? That didn't absolutely positively mean I was signaling my secret admirer that I liked movies.

Then I thought about the possibility that the notes were a trick. What if I showed up in red and everyone started laughing? What would I do then?

I had meant to call my best friends after I finished my homework last night and talk the situation over with them. But I had been so depressed over the way Mom had reacted to her secret admirer note that I had never made the calls. She had talked to me again, before she left for work this morning, about not speaking to strangers and staying away from people who seemed to be just standing around. She was really upset.

Suddenly Keith Masterson's face popped into my mind. He was my secret admirer. I couldn't be more convinced if he had signed his name to those notes. I had to wear red today. I had to let him know that I wanted to go to the movie with him. For a moment I thought about Randy and how Taffy was flirting with him. It made me mad that she was taking advantage of the situation, but if Randy wasn't going to ask me to go to the movie, there wasn't anything I could do.

When I got to school, everything looked normal. Kids were standing in groups talking, and a bunch of boys, including Keith and Randy Kirwan, were racing around the baseball diamond. I breathed a sigh of relief. I hadn't really expected them to be lined up in front of the building just waiting to laugh at me if I showed up wearing red, but I hadn't been certain that they wouldn't, either.

Unfortunately, my feeling of relief didn't last long. I had barely gotten to where my friends were standing near the fence when Taffy Sinclair came marching up to us. Mona Vaughn was following her, naturally, but Alexis and Lisa and Sara were tagging along, too.

"Is it true that you're telling everyone you have a secret admirer?" Taffy challenged.

"I DO have a secret admirer. So what's it to you?"

Taffy just stood there with a nasty look on her face for a moment. Then she smiled confidently at Mona, who said in a meek voice, "Taffy doesn't think the notes are real. She thinks you wrote them yourself."

"What?!" I shrieked. "How dare you say a thing like that, Taffy Sinclair!"

"Everybody knows that Randy hasn't asked you to go to the movie on Saturday," she said. "You want everybody to think that it doesn't matter because somebody else likes you. But it doesn't take brains to figure out that you're faking it."

"Well, if it took brains to figure anything out, you'd be out of luck!" screamed Beth. "You're just jealous because Jana has a secret admirer."

"Ha!" Taffy snickered. "What kind of boy would be her secret admirer, anyway? It would have to be one who liked girls who went around for DAYS with a big fat hole in her hair right by her face."

I could feel my ears getting hot and my face blazing red. Taffy was talking about the time when I forgot to spit my gum out before I went to bed. It got stuck in my hair right above my left ear, and I had to cut it out with scissors. How dare she mention a thing like that! Especially since I had gotten a fabulous new haircut that eliminated the hole completely.

I dug around in my notebook until I found the notes. "See!" I shouted, holding them up in the air. "Here they are. Anybody can see that I didn't write them myself."

"That's because they're typed," Taffy argued, ignoring the notes. "Any kid in the whole school can use the typewriter in the Media Center, so that doesn't prove you didn't write them. You're just boy crazy, Jana Morgan, and you want everybody to think that boys are falling all over themselves for you."

"Oh, yeah?" I blurted. "Well, I know who my secret admirer is, but I'd die before I'd tell you. So THERE!" With that I turned and stomped off toward the building. My friends went with me, leaving Taffy and Mona and all the others standing there.

"Do you really know who it is?" asked Melanie, as soon as we were out of earshot.

"Keith, of course," I said.

"Did he call you or something?" asked Christie.

"No, silly. I told you, he looked at me five times yesterday. It's him, I know it is."

None of my friends said anything to that. I knew they weren't as sure as I was. It didn't matter. Keith would be asking me to the movie soon—probably before today was over—and then they would be convinced.

"I have to stop in the office for a minute before the bell rings," I said, suddenly remembering that Mrs. Winchell wanted to see my notes. "I'll tell you why later. See you guys in class."

I was thinking about Taffy Sinclair when I entered the school. I would show her that I had a real secret admirer if it was the last thing I ever did. I would flirt my head off with Keith Masterson if I had to, and I would make sure he saw that I was wearing red today. I was so busy planning my revenge on Taffy that I almost didn't notice Randy Kirwan at the drinking fountain by the door. He looked up when I walked in and smiled, but for the first time in a long time it wasn't his 1,000-watt smile.

"Hi, Randy," I said, smiling back.

"Hi, Jana," he said shyly. Randy didn't usually act shy, and I couldn't help thinking that he wanted to say something else. It couldn't be about the movie Saturday; Scott had already said he wasn't taking me. Was he trying to tell me that he didn't like me anymore?

I swallowed hard. First Taffy had zeroed in on me, and now it was Randy's turn. I had to get out of there. I didn't want to hear what he was going to say.

"I have to go to the office," I said. I whirled around as fast as I could, not paying any attention to where I was going. Suddenly I smacked into someone and went sprawling across the floor.

"Hey, Jana? Are you okay?"

When I looked up to see who was talking to me, I couldn't believe my eyes. It was Keith Masterson, and he was reaching down to help me up. Not only that, but he had a worried look on his face as if he thought something terrible had happened to me.

"Sure. I'm okay," I said hastily. I felt like such a klutz. "Honest. I'm fine."

The worried look stayed on his face as he helped me to my feet. "Gosh, I'm sorry I bumped into you," he said earnestly. "I guess I wasn't looking where I was going. I'm really glad that you're okay." He was smiling at me, and it may not have been 1,000-watts, but it was close.

After Keith went on, I brushed myself off, thinking about all those movies where violins start playing just before two lovers kiss for the very first time. I had always thought those movies were mushy, but I had almost heard those violins when Keith helped me to my feet. I was more sure than ever that he was my secret admirer. The worried look on his face had proved that.

I had started on down the hall to Mrs. Winchell's office when I suddenly remembered Randy. I glanced back toward the drinking fountain, but he was gone.

11 *

Mrs. Winchell looked up from her work and gave me a friendly smile. "Sit down." She motioned to a chair beside her desk. "I'll be with you in just a moment."

While Mrs. Winchell finished what she was doing, I looked around the office. It was just a regular principal's office with bookshelves on one wall and big windows in the wall by the door so that she could look out into the reception area where Mrs. Lockwood, the school secretary, sat.

Finally Mrs. Winchell pushed the papers aside and looked up at me. "Tell me more about your secret admirer." She was smiling kindly and looking very interested.

"There isn't really much to tell. First, I got this note." I unfolded the first secret admirer note and slid it across the desk to her.

Mrs. Winchell read the note and then asked, "When did you get this one?"

"Tuesday. Right after afternoon recess. Then on Wednesday my friends and I began watching all the boys in class to see who looked at me the most. That's why I know one of them has looked at me five whole times," I said proudly.

Mrs. Winchell smiled. "When did you get the second note?"

"Yesterday, after recess again." I handed her the second note. "Then I found this one stuck in my locker door after school."

Mrs. Winchell studied all three notes. Then she looked at me again. "You must be pretty confident that you know who your secret admirer is and that he's someone you'd like to go to the movies with, since I notice you're wearing red today, just as the note instructs you to do."

I nodded and whispered, "I think it's Keith Masterson."

"Oh," she said knowingly. "Well. He certainly is a nice boy."

"And cute, too." I giggled.

Mrs. Winchell sank back in her chair. I could tell by her expression that she was going to say something else. I was right. "Jana," she began slowly. "I'm not sure exactly how to say this, but I'd like for you to be a little careful about these notes."

Surprise must have shown on my face because she laughed nervously and said, "I don't want to upset you. It's just that . . . well . . . do you remember that I mentioned to you yesterday that you weren't the only one at school who had received a secret admirer note?"

I nodded and tried to swallow, but a big lump was growing in my throat.

"There are certain things about your notes that are similar to the other person's note," she said gently.

"Like what?"

"Well, for one thing, they're all typed on school paper, and also the wording is similar. Two different people probably wouldn't use the same words to express their feelings."

I knew what Mrs. Winchell was saying, but I couldn't believe it. She was saying that someone was really playing a trick on me. That Keith Masterson wasn't my secret admirer after all. I bit my lower lip to keep it from trembling and asked, "Couldn't somebody have gotten the idea from my note? Maybe they wanted to tell someone else that they liked them and just didn't bother to make up new words."

Mrs. Winchell nodded. "That's certainly another possibility," she said kindly. "It's also my responsibility to everyone in this school to make sure no one is doing anything unkind or harmful. I hope you understand that."

I did and nodded to Mrs. Winchell. "Who is the other person getting secret admirer notes?"

Sighing, she said, "I'm afraid I can't tell you that. The other person wants it kept a secret."

A secret? I thought. Then it couldn't be Taffy Sinclair. She would want everybody in the whole wide world to know about it. But who could it be? And who would want to do anything unkind or harmful to this other person and me? I thought about Mom just then, too. I was remembering how paranoid she had gotten when she read her secret admirer note last night. She was sure someone dangerous was out to hurt us, when I was the one who wrote it all along.

That idea made me feel better. Probably Mrs. Winchell was misunderstanding, too. I certainly hoped so. I really wanted Keith Masterson to be my secret admirer and to ask me to go to the movie with him. Probably the other secret admirer just wanted someone to go to the movie with, too.

Mrs. Winchell handed back my notes and said I could leave. I thanked her and was headed for the door when she called my name again. "Jana, there was one more thing I wanted to ask about. Would you sit down again, dear? This will only take a minute."

I sat down on the edge of the chair and waited for her question. She sighed again, as if it was a hard thing for her to ask.

"You were here after school yesterday using the typewriter in the Media Center. Isn't that what you told me?"

I nodded.

"I don't mean to be nosy, but what were you typing? Was it something you couldn't do during the day?"

I tried to look at her, but tears were blurring my sight. I knew what she meant. She thought I had sneaked back after everybody had gone home and typed those notes myself!

"Please, Jana. It's important that you tell me. As you know, the notes were all typed. I'm convinced they were typed on the school typewriter by a student. I don't want to believe that you're the one who typed them, so if you'll just tell me what it was you were typing, we can get this unpleasant business over with once and for all."

"I didn't do it, Mrs. Winchell!" I sobbed. "I told you the truth."

"Okay, Jana. I believe you," she said softly, and handed me a tissue. "I didn't mean to make you cry."

I blew my nose and stared at my left shoe. I still didn't look up when she said again that I could leave, and I scurried out the door. She thought I was the one who wrote the notes. I knew I could never look her in the eye again.

12 ❋

*T*he bell rang as soon as I got out of Mrs. Winchell's office, and I was glad that I had to go straight to class. I certainly didn't feel like talking to anybody. Not even to my four best friends. I was just too depressed. I knew they would be dying to know what I was doing in the principal's office. How could I tell them that she thought I was writing secret admirer notes to myself? And maybe to another person, also? It was just too humiliating.

I sank into my seat and was only partly aware of Wiggins's taking roll and making the morning announcements. I had too many things on my mind to pay attention or even to watch to see which

85

boys were looking at me. What did it matter anyway—if the notes were just a joke? Then I thought about all the times Keith had looked at me and the worried expression he had had when he helped me up in the hall. The notes couldn't be a joke. They just couldn't!

At morning recess my friends were all as chirpy as birds. They had no way of knowing how miserable I felt.

"Did you see how many times Randy Kirwan was looking at you this morning?" cried Beth. She was dancing around excitedly and pointing to her chart. "I saw him three times."

"I saw him twice," said Melanie. She was almost as excited as Beth. "I think he was trying to get your attention."

A rush of hope swept over me for an instant, but it was gone again as I remembered seeing Randy in the hall. He had been trying to get my attention then, too, but from the look on his face I knew he was going to give me bad news.

"He was probably going to tell me that he doesn't like me anymore and that he's taking Taffy out on Saturday," I said dejectedly.

"Jana, how can you say that?" asked Christie in an exasperated voice. "He's your BOYFRIEND!

I'd give anything if Mr. Scott would look at me three whole times in one morning."

I explained to them about seeing Randy in the hall on my way to the office to see Mrs. Winchell and the funny look he'd had on his face. Then I told them about trying to get away before he could say anything and running smack into Keith Masterson.

"I know Keith's my secret admirer." I sounded more confident than I felt. "No matter what Mrs. Winchell thinks."

The moment I said that I knew I had goofed. My friends were looking at me questioningly, and then Christie asked slowly, "What do you mean? What does my mother think?"

"She thinks I sent the notes to myself to get attention and that I even sent a note to someone else." I blurted.

Christie got a horrified look on her face, but she didn't say anything. It was Katie who asked, "She thinks you sent a note to someone else? What are you talking about?"

"There is someone in this school who has gotten a secret admirer note, also. Mrs. Winchell wanted to see my notes to check for similarities. She thinks I wrote all of them because I was using the typewriter after school yesterday and they're all typed. Not only that, but the other letter has some of the same words in it as mine."

"That doesn't prove anything," said Christie.

"I know that," I said, " but SHE thinks it does."

"Who is the other person who got a secret admirer note?" asked Beth.

"I don't know," I confessed. "Mrs. Winchell said the other person wanted it kept a secret."

"That sounds dumb to me," said Melanie. "I'd think she'd want everybody to know."

"At first I thought it might be Taffy Sinclair," I offered. "But you're right, Mel. She'd want everybody in the world to know. But the worst thing is that Mrs. Winchell thinks I've done something terrible, and it's all because of the person who wrote that other note. What am I going to do?"

Beth put an arm around me and gave me a sympathetic hug, but she didn't offer any suggestions. Neither did anybody else. I could see they were as worried as I was.

Christie had been drawing circles in the dirt with the toe of her sneaker. Finally she stopped and said in a tiny voice, "I know who the other person is who has a secret admirer."

"You?!" I cried. "Why didn't you tell us?"

Christie was shaking her head. "It isn't me. It's . . . it's Mr. Scott. I know because I wrote him the note."

I was too flabbergasted to say anything as Christie went on with her story. "It seemed like such a good idea. He never pays any attention to me, and I think he's so wonderful. I wasn't trying to get a date with him or anything. I know that will never happen. I just wanted him to know that somebody really likes him."

"So you copied the first note I got from my secret admirer and left it where he could find it."

Christie nodded. "I wrote, 'Dear Mr. Scott, I am writing to tell you that I have been noticing you for a long time. I think you are very nice and very handsome. I know that you probably like someone else, but I will keep hoping that someday you will like me. Your Secret Admirer.' You've got to believe me, Jana. I had no idea that he would show it to my mother."

Part of me was sympathetic with Christie, but part of me wasn't. "But I'M the one who got in trouble," I insisted.

"Oh, please, PLEASE don't tell on me," Christie begged. "I'll do anything you want me to. You just can't tell her. Okay?"

"Didn't you hear me? I'm the one she thinks wrote all the notes."

"But you didn't," said Melanie. "And when Keith asks you to the movie, you'll have proof that he wrote the ones to you. Mrs. Winchell will believe you then."

"Oh, she will!" said Christie. "I know my mom. She'll believe you."

I sighed, wondering how I ever got myself into these things. "Okay," I said at last. "I'll keep my mouth shut for now, but this had better work out the way you said, Christie. That's all there is to it."

Christie kept bugging me to let her do something to pay me back for not telling her mother the truth. I kept telling her that best friends don't have to pay each other back, but after recess when Wiggins took us to the Media Center for free reading again, I got this great idea.

I was sitting at one of the library tables doodling in my notebook. I was thinking about all the secret admirer notes that had been sent to people since the week began and all the problems they had caused. I shook my head in wonder as I thought about all those notes spreading around like the flu. It was practically an epidemic.

First there were my notes. The first one had made me ecstatic, and so had the second one. Even the third one, the one asking me to wear something red to school today if I liked movies, had been sort of fun at first. But now I wasn't sure I really had a secret admirer, and Mrs. Winchell thought I wrote those notes myself. Then there was the note to Mr. Scott. How could Christie have done something so dumb? Now her mother suspected me of writing it and practically thought I was a criminal. Last was the note I had written to Mom to try to add some excitement to her life. I hadn't meant to frighten her to death.

Still, the more I thought about Mom, the more I realized that the only way I could get her to stop worrying was to write one more note. Just one more. That's all it would take. I glanced over at the typewriter. No one was using it. But what if Mrs. Birney was watching? What if Mrs. Winchell had asked her to report everybody who typed on it? I'd be in more trouble than ever. But nobody suspected Christie, and she'd be glad to do it for me. Especially when I explained about the trouble I had started by writing a secret admirer note to Mom. In a way, Christie and I were in the same boat and could help each other out. I smiled to myself and began deciding what the note would say.

13 ✳

By lunchtime I was beginning to see red. I had been wearing my red jumpsuit all day, not to mention red socks and red barrettes, and Keith had not said one word to me about the movie. After Christie typed the secret admirer note for my mom in the Media Center, I began paying more attention to him. He was looking at me again. I caught him twice before we had to go back to our homeroom. So, why hadn't he said anything to me yet?

The first person I saw when my friends and I got onto the playground after lunch was Taffy Sinclair. She was standing with Mona, and when she saw me she got the biggest smirk on her face I had ever seen.

"I see you're wearing *red* today, Jana," she said in a sarcastic voice.

"I happen to like red. In fact, it's my favorite color."

"I'll bet it is. It's too bad you aren't going to the movie with everybody Saturday."

Her words hit me like a bolt of lightning. I looked at her, and she was still smirking. What did she mean by that? I was dying to ask her, but I didn't dare. When she said everybody, was she including herself? Had my worst fears come true? Did she have a date with Randy?

"I'm going to get a drink," I mumbled, stomping off toward the drinking fountain by the building. I had to get away from there. I was so mad at Taffy Sinclair that if I stayed around her any longer, I didn't know what terrible thing I might do.

As I bent over the fountain, I heard my name.

"Hey, Jana. Can I talk to you a minute?"

It was Keith. He was trotting up behind me, giving me a great big smile. My knees went weak. I could almost hear those violins again.

"Hi, Keith. What's up?" I said as casually as possible.

"There's something I need to ask you," he said, and then I could swear that he almost blushed. My heart was pounding.

"I guess you know a lot of guys are asking girls to go to the movie this weekend?" he asked self-consciously.

I nodded.

"At first, it was just Scott and Joel and Mark who were going on a dare. Joel said Scott didn't have enough nerve to ask Melanie for a real date, and then Scott said Joel didn't have enough nerve to ask Sara, and then they both jumped on Mark to ask Alexis. Stuff like that. Well, anyway, now some more guys are thinking of asking girls, and . . ."

Keith paused as if he was losing his nerve. I thought I'd die. I almost wished I could say the words for him.

He was shifting nervously from one foot to the other. Suddenly he gave me a big grin and blurted, "Do you think Beth would go with me if I ask her?"

You could have knocked me over with one red sock. So that's why he had been staring at me all week. He didn't want to ask *me*. He wanted to ask Beth.

Keith was still talking. "She's your best friend, so you'd probably know if she would go. Do you think I should ask her?"

"Sure. Why don't you talk to her right now? She's over there."

I pointed toward my friends, turning so that Keith could not see the disappointment on my face. I was happy for Beth. Really happy. But what about me?

Beth was delirious when she told me the news a few minutes later. "Oh, Jana," she cried, clutching my arm. "Keith asked me to the movie! He asked ME! He said he talked to you first." Then she paused and got a concerned look. "You aren't mad, are you? I know you thought he was your secret admirer."

"Of course I'm not mad," I said, hugging her. Then I managed to give her a big smile. "I think it's great. I just didn't know that you liked him. Why didn't you tell me?"

Beth looked a little sheepish. "I've always thought he was cute," she admitted, "but then, when you decided he was your secret admirer, I started paying more attention to him. That was when I decided he's not just cute, he's *fantastic*! I didn't want to tell you, though, because I thought he liked you. And Jana," she added, "thanks for not being mad."

How could I be mad at my best friend just because the boy she thought was fantastic had just asked her to go to the movie? It's just that I thought he was cute, too, and now that I had lost Randy, I didn't have anyone.

Beth and Melanie giggled and talked about what they were going to wear Saturday until the bell rang. I tried to join in, but I couldn't. When I got back to my seat, I pulled my chart out of my notebook and drew a line through Keith Masterson's name. If he wasn't my secret admirer, then who was? I had already eliminated Randy and Scott and Mark and Joel. Now Keith was eliminated, too. I'd die if it were Clarence or Curtis or Gregory, so that only left Richie or Eric or Matt. Richie had only looked at me once, and Eric once and a half. I sighed. Matt Zeboski had looked at me four times, just one time less than Keith, but he had only ranked "almost semi-cute" on the cute scale.

Suddenly a terrible thought occurred to me, and I looked up slowly as my eyes focused on the back of Taffy Sinclair's head four seats in front of me. I was remembering what she had said to me on the playground at noon. *I see you're wearing red today, Jana.* How did Taffy Sinclair know that my secret admirer had told me to wear red? I had gotten that note after school and nobody knew about it except my four best friends and Mrs. Winchell.

I racked my brain for a few minutes, trying to figure out how she knew about it. Had one of them slipped and said something in front of her on the playground this morning? I was pretty sure they hadn't as I thought back over the scene before school. She had come up to my friends and me and had accused me of writing the notes myself. I frowned. I did pull them out of my notebook and wave them at her to prove they were real, but she didn't take them or look at them closely. There was no way she could have read the one telling me to wear red.

My heart began to pound. If my friends hadn't slipped, and I was almost positive they hadn't, there was only one other possible explanation. The person who wrote my secret admirer notes was Taffy Sinclair!

At recess I motioned for my friends to follow me to our spot by the fence, where we could talk in private. Then I told them what I suspected.

"Taffy Sinclair is your secret admirer!" Katie shrieked.

She started to laugh, but I gave her a poison-dart look, and she stopped. "Everybody think hard. Did any of you say anything—I mean ANYTHING—that would have tipped off Taffy that my secret admirer told me to wear red?"

My friends all thought for a moment. Then they frowned and shook their heads in unison.

"Then she has to be the one who wrote the notes," I insisted.

"I don't understand why Taffy Sinclair would want you to have a secret admirer instead of her," said Melanie. "You know how conceited she is. Wouldn't you think she'd want all that attention for herself?"

"Yeah," said Beth. "I'd think that if she were going to write fake secret admirer notes, she'd write them to herself."

"I've been thinking about that," I said. "At first I felt the same way you do. But then I thought of something else. Taffy has been trying to take Randy away from me practically forever. She has flirted with him and tried everything she could think of, but nothing worked because he liked me and I liked him."

"So?" asked Christie. "How does sending you secret admirer notes change that?"

"He hasn't asked me to the movie on Saturday, right? So she probably thinks he's losing interest in me. Now, get this. What if I get mad about that? And then what if I find out that I have this fabulous secret admirer? And what if I get carried away with my secret admirer and I lose interest in Randy!

Don't you see? Then Taffy can have Randy all for herself!"

Beth slapped her forehead with the heel of her hand. "That's brilliant, Jana. That has to be it! She even acted jealous to throw you offtrack."

"I agree," said Katie.

"Me, too," said Christie. "Taffy Sinclair is a rat."

"The worst thing is, I WAS getting carried away with my secret admirer," I said. "I got madder and madder at Randy, and if Keith had asked me to the movie, I would have gone. Taffy Sinclair's plan almost worked!"

"But it didn't," said Melanie. "You should be happy about that."

"I won't be happy until I accomplish TWO things," I said. "Get Randy back and get revenge on Taffy Sinclair!"

14 *

*W*hen I got home from school, I planted Mom's second secret admirer note in our mailbox and went to my room to try to figure out what to do about my problems. On the way home I had remembered that there were *three* things I needed to do, not just two. In addition to Randy and Taffy Sinclair, I still had to prove to Mrs. Winchell that I wasn't the one writing the secret admirer notes.

I had thought that when Keith turned out to be my secret admirer, all my troubles with Mrs. Winchell would be over. If I had a real secret admirer, then she would realize that I would never want to write a note to Mr. Scott. But now, Keith had asked Beth to the movie, and Christie had made me promise not to tell on her. I was right back where I started.

A few minutes later I heard Mom come in. I wanted to run in to meet her and see if she had found her note, but I made myself stay where I was. I was afraid I'd give myself away.

"What!" she shrieked an instant later. That was the signal I was waiting for. She had found her secret admirer note.

"What's the matter, Mom?" I asked in fake surprise as I rushed into the living room. She had a sheet of notebook paper in her hand. It was all I could do to keep from grinning.

"I got another one of those *disgusting* notes," she said, her eyes flaring. "Here. Look at this."

She handed the note to me. Even though I knew what it said by heart, I pretended that I was seeing it for the very first time. It said:

Dear Pat,

Please disregard my first note. I had you mixed up with someone else.

Even though you seem like a very nice and very exciting person, you are not the person I meant to write to.

Your former Secret Admirer

"Wow! This is great," I said. "Now we know that nobody is watching us or planning to do anything terrible." I looked at Mom, but she wasn't smiling the way I had hoped she would be. "And look," I added, pointing to the note. "He thinks you're exciting. Isn't that terrific?"

"*Hmmfpt.* Some kind of weirdo, if you ask me," she mumbled as she headed for the kitchen. Still, as she turned to go, I thought I saw the tiniest grin twitching at the corners of her mouth. I breathed a sigh of relief. At least this plan had worked, and she would probably forget all about the notes in a day or two.

When I got back to my room, I started pacing the floor. If only my other problems could be solved as easily. Then I thought about Randy with his beautiful blue eyes and dark, wavy hair. I had to get him back. I just had to! But I still didn't know why he didn't like me anymore or if he was taking Taffy Sinclair to the movie on Saturday. What was even worse, I didn't know what to do.

I considered the possibilities. I could call him and ask him for an explanation. Oh, no, I couldn't, I assured myself quickly. I couldn't do that in a million years! I could have someone else call him— probably Beth—and ask what's wrong. No, that would be almost as terrible as calling him myself. What else? I could ask Melanie to have Scott find out again. I shook my head. I didn't like that idea either. What Scott found out might be too embarrassing. I sighed. I was getting nowhere fast.

I tried and tried to think of another idea. There must be something that I can do, I thought. I knew that whatever it was, it had to be something I did myself. Nobody else could get Randy back for me.

If Mom noticed that I was quiet at dinner, she didn't mention it. I helped with the dishes and then excused myself to do math homework, but I didn't open my book. Instead, I stared at the wall and thought about Randy.

When a soft knock sounded at my bedroom door and Mom called out, "I'm going to run to the store for a couple of things. Back in a few minutes," I knew what I had to do.

I waited until I heard the door close behind her and went into the living room. The telephone sat there on the table by the sofa looking like a big black bug. I didn't want to touch it, but I had to.

I felt tingly all over as I dialed Randy's number and listened to it ring. I didn't have the faintest idea of what I would say. I just knew that I had to talk to him and get things straightened out once and for all.

"Hello," said a masculine voice.

"Randy?" I asked weakly.

"Jana, is that you?" His voice sounded excited.

I nodded nervously, and then I realized he couldn't see that over the phone. "Yes, it's me."

"Great. I was just getting ready to call you. Honest! I was standing right here by the phone getting ready to dial your number."

"You were? Gosh. What did you want to talk to me about?" My heart was pounding, and I sank onto the sofa, clutching the receiver to my ear.

"A couple of things." His voice sounded serious again. Oh, no. I thought. Here it comes. "First, I want to explain why I didn't ask you to the movie, but you've got to promise you won't tell ANYONE."

I frowned, puzzled. "Sure. I promise."

"Well, you see, I have this cousin Julia who was supposed to have this big wedding Saturday, and my parents were making me be in it. They had rented this stupid-looking white tuxedo and a shirt with ruffles on the front, and I was supposed to be a junior groomsman, or something like that. And I was supposed to walk down the aisle with Julia's little sister, who is . . . well, you wouldn't like her. It was going to be gross, and if Scott or Mark or any of my friends ever found out about my wearing a tuxedo and a shirt with ruffles on the front, they'd kid me for the rest of my life."

I wanted to giggle so badly I could hardly stand it as a picture of Randy in a white tuxedo and a frilly shirt popped into my mind. He would look handsome, of course, but he wouldn't look like the Randy I knew. And he was right about his friends. They would never let him live it down.

"I had made up my mind to tell you about the wedding when I saw you in the hall this morning," he went on, "so that you'd understand why I hadn't asked you out. But then you acted as if you didn't want to talk to me. I also know that you have a secret admirer," he said softly. "But I was wondering . . . well . . . if he hasn't already asked you, would you go to the movie with me?"

"What about the wedding?" I burst out.

Randy laughed. "Julia and her boyfriend eloped last night! My parents just found out a few minutes ago, and boy, everybody's having a fit. Aunt Clara fainted. Uncle George hit the ceiling about all the money he had spent on the wedding. What a riot. I think it's great! Now I don't have to go to the wedding and wear that stupid tuxedo. And," he added softly, "I can go to the movie with you, if you'd like to."

"I'd love to!" I said breathlessly. "I really would. And about my secret admirer . . ." I paused and thought a moment. I had started to tell Randy that I didn't really have a secret admirer, but maybe that wasn't such a good idea. "I'd rather go with you," I added quickly.

"Super. So what were you calling me about?"

I swallowed a gasp and thought fast. "Oh, I was just going to ask you which problems we were supposed to do for math homework," I said slyly. "I must have forgotten to write them down."

15 ✳

We talked a little while longer and finally hung up after I promised Randy for the millionth time that I wouldn't tell his friends about the tuxedo. I had just put down the receiver when Mom got home.

"Mom! Guess what! Randy's taking me to the movie on Saturday!" I cried as I jumped up and down.

"Terrific!" she said as she set down the bag of groceries she was carrying and rushed to me, jumping up and down along with me as we hugged. "Tell me all about it."

"Okay. I'll start at the beginning." I collapsed on the sofa and grinned up at her. Then I sat up straight again and began talking as fast as I could. "Well, see, Melanie has this date with Scott for the movie Saturday, and Joel asked Sara, and Mark asked Alexis, but I couldn't figure out why Randy hadn't asked me. Then I got this note from my secret admirer and he . . ." My voice trailed off as I realized what I had just said.

"Ah—HA! So that's where the idea for MY secret admirer came from," she said, and I couldn't tell if she was just joking or if she was really mad. "You wrote those notes, didn't you?"

I nodded mutely and waited for disaster to strike. When Mom didn't say anything right away, I decided I had better explain about that, too. "I didn't mean to scare you or worry you," I insisted. "It's just that your life is so boring, just taking care of me, and going bowling with Pink every Saturday night, and you brought home those travel brochures and said you'd love some excitement and adventure, and I thought . . ." I couldn't say anything more. Tears were gushing into my eyes, and it felt as if something were squeezing my throat.

I heard Mom sigh and felt her arms wrap around me. "And you thought that giving me a secret admirer would add a little excitement and adventure to my life," she said softly. "Oh, Jana. I love you so much." Then she let go of me and tipped my face toward hers so I could see that she was smiling.

Suddenly she was laughing. "Let's get out that mayonnaise jar and start right now to save for a trip." Mom jumped up and ran to the kitchen with me right behind her. Together we washed the jar and dried it and put one dollar and twenty-three cents into it for starters. The twenty-three cents was mine. Then we sat back down on the sofa, and I finished telling her about my date with Randy.

The next morning was Friday, and when I got to school, I marched straight to the office to see Mrs. Winchell. I had made up my mind overnight what to do.

"Good morning, Jana," she said, looking up from some papers on her desk after her secretary had announced me. "How are you this morning?"

"Just fine, thank you. How are you?" I said as politely as I could.

"Very well. Now, what can I do for you?"

"I just thought you might want to know that I was wrong about who my secret admirer was. It wasn't Keith. He asked Beth Barry to go to the movie."

"Oh, I'm sorry."

"That's okay. Randy Kirwan asked me instead. I'm going with him."

"That's wonderful, Jana. Then it was Randy who was your secret admirer, wasn't it?"

"He hasn't said so."

"Well, boys are like that," she assured me. "And I'm sure that the other secret admirer note was just some copycat. I think we can forget about it now."

I was grinning from ear to ear when I left her office. I couldn't help feeling a little guilty, and yet everything I had told her was the truth. Now Christie wouldn't get into trouble either. Everything was working out super.

Then I went looking for Taffy Sinclair. I was ready for her, too. I made a quick stop in our classroom without anyone's seeing me and then headed downstairs to the lockers. Taffy was beside hers, and she had a cluster of girls around her.

"Hi, Taffy," I said as I got near. "Look what I'm wearing today. Blue. Just the way my secret admirer said to do."

Taffy looked startled. She glanced from my face to my jeans and blue sweater and then back to my face again.

"Yup. My secret admirer really knows what he likes for me to wear. Yesterday it was red, and today it's blue."

I could tell that I had shaken her up.

"You're faking," she said. "You don't have a secret admirer."

"Yes, I do!" I insisted. "He left another note in my mailbox yesterday, and boy, you should read it. He said that he's crazy about me, and that I'm the most beautiful girl in the world."

I could tell that I was really getting to Taffy now. Since she had written the first three notes, she couldn't figure out where the last one had come from.

"Let's see it," she demanded.

"Sorry. I left it home for safekeeping."

Just then Christie came up. I had tipped her off about my plan on the phone last night when I had called all my friends to tell them about my date with Randy, and she knew exactly what to do.

"Hi, everybody," she said. "Guess what. I have a secret admirer. Isn't it exciting?"

"Me, too," said Katie, who had walked up from the other end of the hall. "I never realized before just how romantic sixth-grade boys could be."

Taffy was zinging poison-dart looks at each one of us and looking nervously at all the kids standing around listening, but she didn't say a word.

"Gee, Taffy," I said sarcastically. Then in front of everybody I said in a really loud voice, "I'm surprised that you don't have a secret admirer, too."

That was more than Taffy could stand. She whirled away and stomped off down the hall. My friends and I followed her, making sure she didn't see us. When she got to our room, she hurried inside, and we hurried just as fast and peeked in at her. She was reaching for a folded-up note in the middle of her desk. Taffy opened it very slowly, and a smile spread over her face as she read it.

"What does it say?" whispered Melanie.

I gave her a triumphant smile. "It says, 'Dear Taffy, I have been your BIGGEST admirer forever and ever. I think you are totally gorgeous and wonderful. I also think you are the most fabulous person in the whole wide world and even the universe. Your Secret Admirer. P.S. If you want to find out who it is that thinks all these wonderful things about you, look in your desk. I left another note in there.'"

My friends smothered giggles with their hands as we watched Taffy raise the top of her desk. She grabbed the note I had left in there, opened it, and gasped. Then she threw it onto the floor and ran out of the room without even seeing us standing in the hall.

"I have to see what it says, said Beth, running in and picking up the note. She burst out laughing as she read it, then held it up for everyone to see. There were only two words in the middle of the page:

Taffy Sinclair

16 ✻

Scott and his father picked up Joel and Mark and Keith and Randy in the Dalys' big customized van a little after six o'clock on Saturday evening, then picked up all the girls. It was a tight squeeze to get in ten kids and a grown-up, but nobody cared.

I felt a little sad that all of The Fabulous Five wasn't going, even though that would have meant fourteen kids in the van. But Christie had insisted that there wasn't one single boy in sixth grade who could compare with Mr. Scott, and Katie didn't like boys—period. They planned to spend the evening at Christie's, order out pizza from Mama Mia's, and watch a movie on the VCR.

I had spent practically all day getting ready and had talked on the phone to Beth and Melanie three times each, deciding what to wear. Beth kept saying that it wouldn't matter since the movie theater was dark, but I wanted to look just right anyway.

I had finally decided on my lavender pants and matching top, and I could tell by the way Randy looked at me when I opened the door that I had made the right choice. His dark green polo shirt was open at the neck, and his jeans were practically brand-new. He had never looked more handsome in his life!

When we got to the theater, the boys lined up to get the tickets. They horsed around while they waited, laughing and punching each other in the arm, and we girls stood aside, watching them and trying not to giggle.

We ate popcorn and drank soda while we watched the movie, and I had just wiped the salty butter off my fingers when Randy slipped his hand over mine.

I could feel my ears getting warm and my face turning red, but it didn't matter. Everything had worked out perfectly. I didn't need a secret admirer. I had someone who really did like me, and he always had. In fact, in the back of the van on the way home from the movie, he kissed me for the second time.

ABOUT THE AUTHOR

Betsy Haynes, the daughter of a former news-woman, began scribbling poetry and short stories as soon as she learned to write. A serious writing career, however, had to wait until after her marriage and the arrival of her two children. But that early practice must have paid off, for within three months Mrs. Haynes had sold her first story. In addition to a number of magazine short stories and the Taffy Sinclair series, Mrs. Haynes is also the author of *Spies on the Devil's Belt* and the highly acclaimed *Cowslip*. She lives in Colleyville, Texas, with her children and husband, a businessman who is the author of a young adult novel.

The Newest From Taffy Sinclair and the Fabulous Five—Don't Miss Even One!

☐ BLACKMAILED BY TAFFY SINCLAIR

Betsy Haynes   15542-3/$2.50 ($2.95C)

When Jana Morgan finds a wallet in the girls' room at school, she doesn't know it's stolen property. But Taffy does know, and after she catches Jana with the evidence, she gives her a choice. If Jana refuses to become Taffy's personal slave, Taffy will turn her over to the police!

☐ TAFFY SINCLAIR, BABY ASHLEY, AND ME

Betsy Haynes   15557-1/$2.50 ($2.95C)

When archrivals Taffy and Jana find a baby abandoned on the steps of Mark Twain Elementary, their discovery makes them famous overnight and, believe it or not, friends! That is, until Taffy starts taking all the credit and the Fabulous Five must step in to stop Taffy from stealing the show!

TAFFY SINCLAIR AND THE SECRET ADMIRER EPIDEMIC

Betsy Haynes

When Jana gets notes from a secret admirer, she can't figure out who is sending them. But she and her friends discover that the notes are from archrival Taffy Sinclair and the Fabulous Five cook up a plot to put terrible Taffy in her place!

On Sale: February 1988

Bantam Skylark
Means Magical Fun!

☐ **15484-2   BELLA ARABELLA**
  Liza Fosburgh $2.50
When 10-year-old Arabella's stepfather threatens to send her
away to boarding school, she turns to her darling cat Miranda
and whispers "if only I could be a cat like you." Then suddenly,
magically, she becomes one!

☐ **15408   MISS KNOW IT ALL**
  Carol Beach York $2.25
Miss Know It All appears suddenly one morning on the doorstep
of The Good Day Home for Girls. All 28 girls are amazed at all
Miss Know It All knows until something happens to make the
girls fear that they will lose her forever!

☐ **15348   THE DANCING CATS OF APPLESAP**
  Janet Taylor Lisle $2.50
10-year-old Melba Morris likes nothing better than to sit in
Jiggs' Drug Store listening to Mr. Jiggs strum his guitar and
watching the 100 strange and wonderful cats who live there
prance and twirl to the music! But the folks of Applesap must
be convinced that the cats are not evil, and Melba is the only
one who can do that!

Prices and availability subject to change without notice.